Grandma's Vietnamese to English Dictionary:

bà [*baa*]: grandma

bánh tráng nướng [*hahn trang new-ung*]: grilled rice paper

cám ơn [*gahm uhn*]: thank you

chào [*ch(j)ow*]: hello

cháu [*ch(j)au*]: grandchild

không sao [*kohng sao*]: it's okay; no problem

For my family, and for all those who have the courage to learn a new language—A.P.K.

For my nephews, Gôn and Gíp—D.H.

Words Between Us
Text copyright © 2023 by Angela Pham Krans
Illustrations copyright © 2023 by Dung Ho
All rights reserved. Manufactured in Italy.
No part of this book may be used or reproduced in any manner whatsoever without written permission except in the case of brief quotations embodied in critical articles and reviews. For information address HarperCollins Children's Books, a division of HarperCollins Publishers, 195 Broadway, New York, NY 10007.
www.harpercollinschildrens.com

Library of Congress Control Number: 2022931769
ISBN 978-0-06-322454-4

The artist used Adobe Photoshop to create the digital illustrations for this book.
Typography by Chelsea C. Donaldson
23 24 25 26 27 RTLO 10 9 8 7 6 5 4 3 2 1
First Edition

Words Between Us

Written by **Angela Pham Krans** Illustrated by **Dung Ho**

HARPER

An Imprint of HarperCollinsPublishers

Felix and Grandma had lived oceans apart,
but today was the day Grandma arrived.
When he finally saw her, he said hello, "Chào bà."
And she said hello, "Chào cháu."
It was the first time they met.

CHÀO MỪNG BÀ ĐẾN MỸ

Felix made Grandma a special dinner. It was his favorite food.
"Peet suh," Grandma said. It was her first meal in America
and the first English word Felix taught her.

Grandma moved into the room across from Felix's. Day after day, as Felix got to know Grandma, Grandma got to know Felix.

He gave her a tour of the city.

She gave him a tour of her village.

He taught her how to play the drums.
She taught him songs she sang as a child.

He showed her how
to care for Pete.

She showed him how to care
for their garden.

One day, Felix took Grandma to the city's biggest festival.
They ate food on sticks and slurped drinks with fancy umbrellas.

FUNNEL CAKES

FRIED DOUGH

COLD DRINKS

ELEPHANT EARS

FOOD ON A STICK

HOT DOGS

DEEP-FRIED OREOS

Ice Cream

CANDY APPLES

SNO-CONES

CANDY LAND

SUNDAES SH

But the festival was getting too loud and too crowded.
And when Felix wasn't paying attention, he lost Grandma.

Felix asked for help.

Grandma didn't know
how to ask for help.

Finally, there she was.

"Bà, were you scared?" Felix asked.
Grandma nodded.

Felix hugged Grandma, and
Grandma hugged Felix.

Felix didn't like Grandma being scared,
but he didn't know how to help her.
"People were very nice, but they didn't
understand me," Grandma said in Vietnamese.

"Bà, do you want to learn English?" Felix asked. "I can help."

Grandma nodded.

Felix taught Grandma the important words first.

Cheese

Chee

Then mom and dad suggested other words.

Some words were funny.

Some words
were frustrating.

When Grandma stumbled, Felix held her hand
and whispered, "Không sao." It's okay.

Felix helped Grandma collect more words.

Grandma studied them every night.
As she tucked Felix into bed, she whispered,
"Cám ơn." Thank you.

Words became phrases. And phrases became sentences.

"Hello, my name is Lan,"
Grandma said in English.

"Can you please help me?"

"We grow good food."

Grandma could say many things now.
They spoke in Vietnamese. They spoke in English.

"Where is Pete?"

"Pete is gone."

But sometimes, they didn't need to say anything at all.

Grandma picked up a flashcard.

"Do you want to cook a peet suh?" she asked.

Felix nodded.

Grandma went to the garden to pick the ingredients.
When she came back, she had herbs and vegetables and an . . .

"Igwana!"

Pizza was Felix's favorite food, but this time
Grandma made it a little differently.
"Bà, what do you call this?" Felix asked.

"Vietnamese peet suh!"

Vietnamese pizza, also known as bánh tráng nướng, is a popular snack sold at food stalls in Vietnam. The pizza is made with rice paper, eggs, and any of your favorite toppings. The rice paper is traditionally grilled, but you can make it at home using a pan or skillet.

Do you want to try Grandma's favorite Vietnamese pizza? Ask an adult to help you make this recipe.

Quả chanh
Lemon

Tỏi
Garlic

Here are the ingredients you'll need:

- 1 egg
- 1 tbsp chopped scallions
- 1 sheet rice paper
- 2 tbsp grated cheese (cheddar and jack cheese blend)
- 6–8 pepperoni slices
- 1/3 cup pulled pork

Let's make a "peet suh"!

Crack the egg into a bowl and whisk it with the chopped scallions.

Heat a pan on low heat. The pan should be large enough to fit the sheet of rice paper.

Place the rice paper in the pan and pour the egg mixture on top. Using the back of a spoon, spread the egg mixture to the edges of the rice paper. This will help flatten out the rice paper.

Once the egg mixture starts to set (about 30 seconds), add the cheese, pepperoni, and pork.

Continue to cook the rice paper until crispy (about 2–3 minutes). Then remove it from the pan.

Cut the pizza into slices to share with your family or fold it in half and eat it all by yourself!